BY JUDITH PRANSKY ★ ILLUSTRATED BY SARAH ZEE

# MISTER LISTER

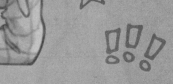

1. TAKE A DEEP
   BREATH .

2. PUT A SMILE
   ON YOUR FACE.

Menucha Publishers, Inc.
© 2018 by Judith Pransky

Typeset and designed by Deena Weinberg
All rights reserved

ISBN 978-1-61465-653-1
Library of Congress Control Number: 2017915240

Published and distributed by:
Menucha Classroom Solutions
An imprint of Menucha Publishers, Inc.
1235 38th Street
Brooklyn, NY 11218
Tel/Fax: 718-232-0856
www.menuchapublishers.com
sales@menuchapublishers.com

0422/B1862/A8

Printed in USA

Dedicated to those
children and adults who
"just want to fit in."

# Contents

### Chapter 1

# TODAY'S THE DAY!

**R**euven was wide awake before his alarm had a chance to buzz. He was smiling, even though his stomach was doing nervous flips.

"Today's the day!" he announced to the empty room. He jumped out of bed and threw on the new school clothes he had set out the night before. Then he raced to the kitchen with his shirt half tucked in. His curly hair sprang out around his head making his *kippah* slide over one ear.

"Oops!" He skidded to a halt. "Forgot to make my bed."

Reuven dashed back to his bedroom. He dragged

the blue-checked blanket across his bed, leaving the other half on the floor. He shoved his pajamas under the pillow, then ran back to the kitchen, still ignoring the hairbrush sitting on his dresser.

"Good morning, Ima!" he shouted, bursting into the kitchen. He flung his arms around his mother. "Today's the day!"

"It certainly is," Ima agreed with a smile and in a much quieter voice. She tried to keep her balance in Reuven's wild hug. "Your first day of third grade in a new school and a new city."

She unlocked Reuven's arms from around her waist. "Remember we talked about not running into people?" she asked. "Or hugging them so hard that you hurt them?" She patted down his curly hair and told him to tuck in his shirt. Then she took a hair clip out of her pocket and clipped his *kippah* in place.

"Where's Abba?" Reuven asked, looking around for his father.

"He already left for work," Ima said, while Reuven sat down at the table. "He's starting his new job today. But he wishes you good luck."

"Hi, everyone," Reuven's older sister Shira yawned as she entered the kitchen.

"Today's the day!" Reuven yelled.

"Ow!" Shira covered her ears. "Ima, can't you get him to quiet down?" She glared at Reuven. "Don't give me a headache on my first day of fifth grade in a new school."

Shira slid into a chair. She smoothed her crisp white blouse and gray pleated skirt. She reached for the cereal box while Reuven picked up pieces that had slid across the table.

"How soon do we have to leave?" she asked her mother.

"In about fifteen minutes," Ima answered. "The school's on Maple Avenue, which is only about a ten-minute drive from here."

"Maple is right after Spruce," Reuven said. He poured too much milk into his cereal and some of it splashed on the table.

"How do you know that?" Shira asked him. "We just moved here a few days ago!"

Reuven shrugged. "And Spruce comes after Walnut. Then comes Chestnut and Cherry and Elm." He shoveled cereal into his mouth. Some of it dripped onto his shirt.

Shira stopped eating. She stared at her brother. "Come on, Reuven," she said. "How do you know all that?"

"I'm wondering the same thing," Ima said. "Tell us how you know."

Reuven shrugged again. "You drove us over to see the school yesterday," he said to his mother. "I was looking at all the street signs." He took another mouthful of cereal. "I made a list in my head and I asked Abba about it last night. He told me they're all names of trees. And he said there's another Jewish school on Chestnut, but it's not Orthodox, like the one we're going to on Maple."

"That's pretty amazing," Shira said.

Reuven turned to her. "After Elm, there are some names of flowers, like — "

"Okay, Mister Lister," Ima interrupted him. "Stop talking with your mouth full and finish eating. You'll be late for your first day." She leaned over to clean the cereal spots on his shirt with a damp rag. Then she wiped off the table and dried the floor around his seat.

Half an hour later, Ima pulled their bright blue van into the carpool line at the Torah Day School on Maple Avenue. Reuven was smiling nervously and his stomach was flip-flopping again.

"So many people," Shira said, her face pressed against the window. "It was a lot quieter when we came here yesterday."

A teacher came over to the van. He showed Shira and Reuven where all the classes were meeting. Shira kissed her mother good-bye and walked toward the girls' building. But Reuven stayed in the van.

"What grade are you in?" the teacher asked kindly.

"Third," Reuven said.

"See that tall man over there?" The teacher pointed toward a young man in a white shirt. He was holding up a sign with a giant number 3 on it. Children gathered around him.

"It's so noisy," Reuven whispered, his eyes wide. "I don't like all this noise." He covered his ears with his hands.

"It will be okay," Ima said. "Once you get into your classroom, it will be quieter."

"Your mother is right," the teacher agreed. "You'll only be out here for a short time. Everything will be much calmer inside."

"In our old school, Shira was in the same building," Reuven said to his mother. "She used to walk me to my classroom."

"You're in third grade now," Ima said. "And this school is bigger, so the girls have their own building. They're not just in separate classes like they were in your old school. I showed you that yesterday." Reuven didn't answer and Ima said, "You'll see Shira when I pick you both up later."

Reuven still didn't move, and Ima said, "Let's make a list like we always do when you're nervous about something."

1. Take a deep breath and go over to your teacher.

2. Put a smile back on your face.

3. Have a great day.

Slowly, Reuven slid out of the van. He made his way through the crowd to join his group. The tall young teacher turned to him and held out his hand. "Good morning, young man. I'm Rabbi Goodman. Who are you?"

Chapter 2

# THE NAME GAME

Reuven glanced back at Ima driving away. He took another deep breath, smiled, and gave his name. Then he grabbed Rabbi Goodman's outstretched hand tightly and shook it...and shook it...and shook it.

"Whoa!" Rabbi Goodman laughed. He took his hand away from Reuven and shook out his fingers. "You've got quite a grip there, but I've only got one right hand. Let's make sure I can still use it." He smiled before checking off Reuven's name on the clipboard. Then he turned to greet two more boys.

When they all were there, Rabbi Goodman led his twenty third-graders into the building. They went up a wide marble staircase and through freshly painted hallways to Room 203. The walls of the room were covered with bright posters. The desks were in a large semicircle.

"Everyone take the seat closest to you. We're going to get to know each other," Rabbi Goodman called out when the students stepped inside.

Most of the boys already knew each other from second grade. There was a mad rush as children tried to grab seats near their friends. Reuven and two other new boys were starting to sit down when Rabbi Goodman came over. He said, "How about if you three help me give out these cards and markers?"

He handed baskets of markers to the other two boys. He handed a stack of large cards in many different colors to Reuven. The new boys walked from desk to desk to pass out markers and cards. Each of the seated boys took some time to choose just the right color marker.

They fingered Reuven's cards to find just the right color. Reuven tried to fan out the cards in his hands so they could see all the colors. He'd seen Shira do that with playing cards. But these cards were large and stiff, and there were too many of them. When the next boy grabbed a card from the center, Reuven lost his hold and the entire stack showered to the floor. A few boys snickered.

Rabbi Goodman crouched next to Reuven to help him pick up the cards. "Hey, what happened to that strong grip of yours that almost broke my hand?" Rabbi Goodman joked. But when Reuven did not give him an answering smile, he said quickly, "There are only a few more cards to give out. I'll do it. Why don't you take a seat?"

When everyone had a card and markers, Rabbi Goodman said, "Okay, gang. We're making name cards so everyone will know everyone else, including the new boys." He folded a card in half and propped it on his desk. "Fold your cards like this one so you can stand it up on your desk. Then use the markers to write your first name in large, clear Hebrew letters on one side of the card. Make sure everyone around the room can see it."

The class grew very quiet for a few minutes. All the boys concentrated on writing big, perfect letters. Reuven chewed his bottom lip and tried his best to write neatly, but markers never drew what he pictured in his mind. He wrote the first three Hebrew letters of his name — resh, for the "re" sound, and aleph and vav for the "u" sound. Then he realized he had almost no space left on the card. He had to squeeze in the last two letters as best he could — vet for the "ve" sound and nun for the "n" sound.

"Stand up your cards when you're done," Rabbi Goodman told them. He walked around the semicircle, adjusting the cards to make sure they could be seen. "Wow! We've got an artist in this class," he exclaimed, holding up the card of one of the new boys. The boy's name was Tzvi. He smiled as everyone admired the fancy lettering he'd used for his name. Colorful stars and swirls surrounded it. But Reuven glanced worriedly at his own squiggly and squashed letters.

"Now, here's the next step in getting to know each other," Rabbi Goodman announced, leaning his tall body against his desk and facing the boys. "I want you all to think of something that makes you special." He looked from face to face around the room. "Are you an artist, like Tzvi? Are you a fast runner? Do you like to read? Do you love animals? Are you super strong?"

He let them all think about it for a moment. Then he said, "Make it into a riddle for the class to guess and try to draw a picture of your riddle on the other side of your card. For example, for me, I'd say, 'I'm like a giraffe,' and I'd draw a picture of a giraffe on my card. Can anyone figure out what I mean?"

"You're so tall!" Reuven shouted, together with a few other boys. He bounced up and down in his seat and laughed.

"You got it!" Rabbi Goodman smiled. "But next time, all of you say it just loud enough for this class to hear, instead of the whole school." A few boys laughed. Rabbi Goodman continued, "Let's see what riddles you can come up with."

## Chapter 3

# REUVEN'S RIDDLE

The room became even quieter than before. Each boy thought about himself and tried to create a really good riddle for the class. Slowly, one after another, boys picked up their markers and began drawing pictures on their cards. But Reuven just sat. He wasn't a fast runner. He didn't love animals. He wasn't as strong as his sister Shira. He liked to read books, but his mother always said he should read more. He wasn't very tall or very short. He certainly wasn't an artist. What made him special?

"Who wants to start?" asked Rabbi Goodman.

Two boys raised their hands. Rabbi Goodman peered at the name card of the one closest to him. "Okay, Moshe. What's your riddle? What did you draw?"

Moshe held up his card. It had a brown blob on it. "It's supposed to be a brown bear," he said, "but I can't draw."

"A brown bear," Rabbi Goodman echoed. "Can anyone guess what that means? Why does Moshe think he's like a brown bear?"

"He's big and strong like a bear," a boy named Shimon called out. But Moshe shook his head.

"He's cuddly, like a teddy bear," Tzvi said. Everyone laughed, but Moshe shook his head.

"I know!" exclaimed Ephraim, who was sitting next to Reuven. "Bears like to sleep a lot. I read a book about a bear sleeping all winter. Is that it?"

Everyone looked at Moshe, who smiled sheepishly and nodded. "I never like to get up in the morning. My mother even had a lot of trouble waking me up for school today."

"Good job!" exclaimed Rabbi Goodman. "You guessed it, Ephraim, so you're next."

Ephraim had drawn a worm on his card. Tzvi guessed it was a bookworm, because Ephraim loved to read. Then everyone admired Tzvi's drawing of a deer and found out he was a very fast runner. He also told the class that his name was Hebrew for "deer."

There was a picture of a cat for a boy who loved milk, especially milkshakes. There was a picture of waves for a boy who loved to swim. But Reuven still couldn't think of a riddle for himself, and now finally it was his turn. Rabbi Goodman bent down and peered at his card.

"I forgot your name. You are..." He squinted at the card but couldn't read it. Some boys tried to help out, but no one could get past the first letter — *resh*.

Reuven heard whispers and giggles in the room. "It says Reuven," he said softly.

"Right. I remember now," said Rabbi Goodman, straightening. "What's your riddle, Reuven?"

Hurriedly, Reuven made a few scribbles on the back of his card and held it up.

"What's that?" a tall boy named Amos asked loudly.

"It's supposed to be writing," said Reuven miserably. "Lines of writing."

"You like to write?" one of the boys asked.

"But no one can read it," someone else said. Everyone laughed.

"Reuven, I think you'd better tell us your riddle because it's almost time for recess," Rabbi Goodman said quickly.

"It's a list," Reuven said. "My Ima calls me 'Mister Lister' because I remember things, long lists of things, like — "

Just then the bell rang for recess, so no one heard

Reuven say the words "street signs." Instead, they lined up near the door to go out to the schoolyard. Reuven heard a few boys repeating "Mister Lister" over and over.

## Chapter 4

# RECESS RACES

**F**irst-graders played on the swings and slides and jungle gym. Older boys took over the basketball court. Rabbi Goodman led his students to a grassy, open area of the schoolyard. Several teachers stood in the shade of a tree, talking, and Rabbi Goodman walked over to them. The boys lingered nearby, deciding how to use their free time.

"Hey, Tzvi, I'll race you to the fence," Shimon called out. He pointed to the schoolyard fence about 40 feet away.

"Me too!" shouted Moshe.

"And me!" yelled Amos.

Reuven watched with envy as six boys formed a crooked starting line facing the fence. He would have loved to be part of their group, but whenever he tried to really speed, he somehow tripped over his own feet.

"We need someone down at the fence to judge who touches it first," Amos said, looking around.

"Me!" Reuven called out eagerly, at the same time as a red-haired boy named Levi. Reuven moved very close to Amos and tugged on his sleeve. "Me!" he repeated. "I can do that!"

"So can I," Levi said, looking hopefully at Amos.

"Me! Me!" Reuven insisted. Amos tried to step away from Reuven. Reuven tugged harder and harder on Amos's sleeve.

"You're going to rip my brand-new shirt!" Amos yelled. He tried to shake free of Reuven's tight grip. "My Ima's going to be mad!" He shoved Reuven, who tripped over Levi's foot and went sprawling on the grass.

"What's happening here?" Rabbi Goodman cried, running over and helping Reuven up. "Why did you push him?" he demanded of Amos.

"He started it!" Amos yelled. "He was going to rip my brand-new shirt!"

"I wasn't ripping it," Reuven said, his lips trembling. "I just wanted to..."

"It would've ripped in another minute!" Levi chimed

in. "He grabbed Amos's shirt and kept pulling it and pulling it!"

"Okay, everyone. Calm down," Rabbi Goodman said more quietly. He called over one of the other teachers. "I need to talk to Reuven privately and then to the other boys," Rabbi Goodman told him. "Can you watch this group and bring them in after recess?"

The other teacher nodded.

Rabbi Goodman took Reuven to the resource room. It was large and very quiet after the noisy schoolyard. Only the resource room teacher, Mrs. Silver, was there. Reuven could hear the shouts of the other children through the open windows. He wished he were outside with them. This was what always happened in his old school. He just wanted to be part of the group, but something always seemed to go wrong. He could feel tears prickling his eyes, but he was determined not to cry. He didn't want Rabbi Goodman to think he was a baby.

"Let's sit down," Rabbi Goodman said. He pointed at a table in the far corner. Above it was a picture of apples and honey, reminding everyone that Rosh Hashanah was coming. Rabbi Goodman and Reuven sat down facing each other.

"Tell me what happened out there," Rabbi Goodman said. He sounded kind.

Reuven swallowed and took a deep breath, hoping his voice would sound normal. "I wanted to be the judge for the race." His voice was shaky. He took another deep breath to steady it. "Levi wanted to be the judge, too. So I was asking Amos to pick me."

"How were you asking?" Rabbi Goodman wanted to know.

Reuven shrugged. "I was just asking."

"Can you show me?"

Reuven looked confused.

"How about if we act it out," Rabbi Goodman suggested. "I'll be Amos, and you show me what happened with his shirt."

Reuven stood up hesitantly. He moved near Rabbi Goodman and touched his sleeve.

Rabbi Goodman laughed. "If that's all you did, Amos wouldn't have even known you were there! Come on, Reuven. Tug on the shirt the way you did in the schoolyard."

Reuven gave a half-smile. He took hold of a handful of Rabbi Goodman's sleeve. He tugged it gently.

"And what did you say?" asked Rabbi Goodman.

"Pick me. Pick me," Reuven said softly.

Rabbi Goodman sat quietly for a few minutes, lost in thought. Reuven let go of his shirt. He stood first on one foot, then the other. He stared longingly at the screens and guardrails of the open windows, wishing he were on the other side. Then Rabbi Goodman said, "I have an idea. Let's change places." Reuven looked confused again, so Rabbi Goodman explained. "You be Amos and I'll be you."

"But...but..." Reuven stammered. "But I'm not a fast runner. I couldn't be in the race."

Rabbi Goodman smiled reassuringly. "You're not running anywhere. We're just acting out the shirt part again."

He told Reuven to stand where he was, then Rabbi Goodman stepped close to him. He bent down and tugged on Reuven's shirtsleeve. "Pick me, Amos. Pick me!" he called. He tugged again. "Pick me. Pick me," Rabbi Goodman repeated.

Reuven wanted to push him away, but he would never do that to a teacher. "Please stop," he whispered.

Rabbi Goodman stopped immediately. He sat down on the chair again. "Why did you want me to stop?" he asked gently.

"I don't know," Reuven said helplessly, looking at the floor. "It was just... I didn't like it. I don't know."

"Was I standing too close to you?" Rabbi Goodman asked. "Did you want me to move away?"

Reuven nodded.

"Do you think Amos might have felt the same way?"

Reuven thought about that. He slowly nodded again.

## Chapter 5

# GIANT STEPS

The other third-graders came back from recess a short while later. Reuven was sitting at his desk and Rabbi Goodman was writing on the board. As they passed Reuven, a few boys stared at him wide-eyed. Someone whispered, "Did he punish you?"

Reuven smiled. He whispered back, "No. We just talked."

The boys settled into their seats. Rabbi Goodman came around to the front of his desk and leaned against it. It was time for *davening*, morning prayers, but he wanted to do something else first.

"Before we *daven*, who can tell me what I wrote on the board?" he asked.

Half the class raised their hands. He pointed to Ephraim, who said, "You wrote your name — Rabbi Shalom Goodman."

"Correct," Rabbi Goodman said. "And how did I write it?"

More hands went up. Moshe said, "You put stars around the 'Shalom' part."

"Why do you think I did that?" Rabbi Goodman asked. "Think carefully," he added. "It's not because I like my first name so much that I wanted to make it fancy."

Tzvi raised his hand slowly. "*Shalom* means 'hello' and 'good-bye'. And doesn't it also mean 'peace'? Is that why you wrote it like that?"

"You're on the right track," Rabbi Goodman replied. "Everybody think about the third meaning Tzvi gave. Peace. It's my name, so peace is really important to me." He let them all consider that for a minute. Then he asked Reuven and Amos to come to the front of the room.

"They need to shake hands and have *shalom* between them. Right?" Shimon asked.

"Well...yes. But not just yet," Rabbi Goodman told the class. "First, they're going to put on a little skit for you."

Reuven and Amos looked at Rabbi Goodman uneasily. "What are we supposed to do?" Amos asked.

Rabbi Goodman stood between the boys. "You're going to act out what happened outside during recess," he told them. "But you're going to think about the mistakes you both made the first time. You're going to figure out how to make it end differently."

"How was the first day of school?" Abba asked Reuven and Shira at the supper table that evening.

"Really good," Shira said, spooning lasagna and salad onto her plate. "I made friends with two girls. One of them is going to call me after supper to work on our homework together. And I really like my English teacher."

After they all filled their plates, they stopped talking as they always did before beginning a meal. Each of them had to say a *brachah*, a blessing, before starting to eat. Abba went first. He made one type of *brachah* for the lasagna and a different one for the salad. The rest of the family said, "Amen." Then Ima said the same two *brachot* for her food, and Shira and Reuven repeated the blessings for theirs.

As they continued eating, Abba turned to Reuven. "How about you?" Abba asked Reuven.

Reuven shrugged. He stared at a puddle of tomato

sauce. It had dripped off his plate onto the table. "A boy pushed me at recess, and I fell," he mumbled.

"Did you get hurt?" Ima asked. Reuven shook his head. "Weren't there teachers around?" Ima asked.

Reuven nodded. "Rabbi Goodman — he's my Hebrew teacher. I really like him. He helped me get up. Then he took me inside and we talked about it." Reuven took a forkful of lasagna. A glob dropped onto his pants. "When the other boys came in, we did a skit about it," he said. His mouth was full, and he sounded much happier. "Just me and Amos, the boy who pushed me. It was fun!"

Ima looked across the table at Abba and smiled. "I was told this Rabbi Goodman is a good teacher," she said.

When they finished eating, Ima asked Shira to clear the dinner plates and put out dessert plates. Then Ima went to get the special dessert she had bought in honor of the first day of school. She came back with a box of cupcakes. Each one was decorated with different colored icing and different mini candies sprinkled on top.

"Oooooh," Shira crooned. She stepped near her mother's seat and stared at the assortment. "They look scrumptious! Which one do I pick?"

Reuven jumped up from his seat and raced around the table. He squeezed between Ima and Shira and leaned over the box.

"Don't push!" Shira said, annoyed. "You're always pushing me." She turned to her mother. "Ima, will you *please* get him away from me!"

Ima sighed and opened her mouth to speak to Reuven. But before she could say anything, Reuven straightened and took a giant step backward. "Sorry," he said to Shira. "I forgot about the giant step."

Shira stared at him. "Giant step?"

"From the skit," Reuven told her. "With Amos, after recess. Rabbi Goodman told us to figure out how to change what happened in the schoolyard."

"How did you change it?" Abba asked.

Reuven looked across the table at his father. "Amos told me he didn't like standing so close together. That was what he changed instead of pushing me. And I took a giant step away from him."

Ima laughed delightedly. She grabbed Reuven and gathered him onto her lap. "We're going to get very close together right now," she said. She hugged him tightly and kissed his hair. "I hope you don't mind."

The next morning, when Reuven and Shira sat down for breakfast, there was a blue and silver cereal box on the table.

"You bought us something new," Shira said to her mother, looking at the box. "Shooting Stars."

Ima nodded. "In honor of your second day of school."

"Thank you. Looks good." Shira poured some into her bowl but didn't start to eat. "Which *brachah* are we supposed to say for it?" she asked.

"Hmm," Ima said. "I'm not sure. It all depends on what it's made from." She picked up the box to read the ingredients. "I'm still not sure," she murmured. "But I have a *brachot* list that I got when I registered you at school. It has the names of different cereals and the *brachot* to say before eating them. There was a stack of lists on a table in the school office."

She found the list on a small pile of papers on the kitchen counter and began reading it.

"The *brachah* for Shooting Stars is *shehakol!*" Reuven called out, using the first Hebrew word of one of the blessings. He was pouring too much milk into his bowl again. As usual, some of it splashed on the table.

Shira turned to her mother. "Is he right?"

Ima looked down the list and nodded. She read the full blessing. "*Shehakol niheyeh bidvaro.*" It meant that all things are created by God.

"How did you know that?" Shira asked Reuven. "But I guess I shouldn't be wondering — not after that business yesterday with all the street names!"

Reuven shrugged his shoulders. "I saw the paper on the counter. I like looking at lists."

"Of course," Shira said, rolling her eyes.

Reuven said the *brachah* and took a mouthful of

cereal. He barely swallowed before saying in a sing-song voice, "Shooting Stars is *shehakol*. Cheerios is *mezonot*. Corn Chex is *ha'adamah*. Cocoa Puffs is — "

"He memorized the whole list!" Shira exclaimed in amazement.

"Okay, okay, Reuven," Ima laughed. "You've made your point. Now finish eating."

Chapter 6

# STUDY PARTNERS

**W**eeks passed. The special holidays of Rosh Hashanah and Yom Kippur were celebrated. Then Reuven's family built a cozy hut in their backyard to celebrate the harvest-time holiday of Sukkot. This was Reuven and Shira's favorite holiday because it was like going camping. They ate all their meals in the Sukkah, the hut. And if the weather cooperated, they sometimes took sleeping bags outside and spent the night in it with Abba. Ima always preferred her own bed indoors.

The days grew cool and crisp. The leaves on the

schoolyard trees turned red and gold and orange. At recess, Reuven liked to sit under a large tree near the fence. The tree spread its branches like a giant umbrella, and its leaves fell down around Reuven like multicolored snow.

Reuven chose that tree because it was close to the Recess Races finish line. The races took place every few days, and Reuven always watched. He liked to watch even though he wasn't fast enough to join.

There was another reason Reuven liked sitting near the finish line. Once in a while the boys chose him to judge the winners. He watched carefully to see who came in first, second, and third. But only when Levi or Ephraim, the regular judges, weren't there.

"Tzvi's in the lead," he told Ima and Shira one day in early November. They were in the van, on the way home from school. "He's always in the top three. He came in first ten times. He was second eleven times. And he was third only twice."

"He's the fastest in the class?" Ima asked.

"Uh-huh," Reuven said. "Amos is next, but he's way behind Tzvi. He's six, six, and seven. And Moshe is behind him with four, five, and five."

"They keep a chart?" Ima asked.

"No," Reuven said.

"Then how do you know all that?" Shira asked in wonder.

Reuven shrugged. "I just know it. I watch them all the time. I like to make lists in my head."

"Here we go again! My brother, Mister Lister," Shira said with admiration. "Boy! If only I had a memory like yours. Then I wouldn't have to spend so much time studying for my vocabulary test."

The next morning, "Brachot Bee" was on the classroom board in giant letters. Rabbi Goodman looked at the boys.

"Anybody know what this means?" he asked. "Does anyone know what a bee is?"

Half the class went, "Bzzzzzzz," and everyone laughed.

"It's also a competition," Rabbi Goodman explained. He moved from behind his desk and walked around their semicircle. "A contest. We're going to have one in school. I'll tell you all about it, but first let's talk about brachot — blessings. You all know what they are, but why do we say them?"

"It's a way of saying thank you," Ephraim said.

"Right. But for what?" Rabbi Goodman asked.

"For our food," Levi answered. "Everything we eat and drink."

"You're right, too," said Rabbi Goodman. "We say thank you to God, to Hashem. But is it only for food and drink? Do we say thank you for anything else?"

Other hands went up and Rabbi Goodman called

on Tzvi. "There's a *brachah* for new clothes. We say thank you for that, too."

"Good! What else?" Rabbi Goodman asked.

"Seeing lightning!" Amos called out.

"And hearing thunder!" Shimon chimed in.

"And candles. Lighting candles for Shabbat," Moshe added.

"Terrific!" Rabbi Goodman exclaimed. "We show appreciation for the great things we have in this world and for special things we do — like seeing an ocean or a rainbow."

"I saw a rainbow once," Reuven said. "But I didn't know there was a *brachah* for that."

"I'm sure a lot of people don't know about that *brachah*," Rabbi Goodman said. "Or which brachah to say for what. Like cereals. You eat them all the time. But each one has a different *brachah*, depending on what they're made from."

Reuven remembered his mother saying the same thing when Shira asked about the *brachah* for the Shooting Stars cereal.

"That's what the Brachot Bee is for," Rabbi Goodman continued. "To see which classes in Torah Day School know the *brachot* best. And there are prizes for the winners."

An excited murmur went around the room. "The first and second grades compete against each other," Rabbi Goodman explained. "The third and fourth grades compete against each other. The fifth and sixth grades compete, and the seventh and eighth. Each winning class gets a pizza and ice cream party on Hanukkah!"

A cheer went up. All twenty boys began talking and shouting at once. Rabbi Goodman held up his hand. His middle three fingers were extended. The boys knew what that meant. Those fingers stood for the Hebrew letter *shin*, and *shin* stood for *sheket*, the Hebrew word for "quiet." The noise stopped.

"Let me explain how this works," Rabbi Goodman said. He looked around at all the eager faces. "First, each class has its private Brachot Bee. We end up with five winners. Those five are the class representatives. They compete for our class against the five winners from the fourth grade."

"Ephraim, you'll be one of the five," Amos called across the room.

"And Levi," Tzvi said.

"You will too, Tzvi," Levi told him.

"We'll see," Rabbi Goodman said. "Every one of you has a chance. We're having our class bee in three weeks, at the end of November. We'll study different groups of *brachot* each week to prepare."

That night, the entire supper conversation was about the Brachot Bee. There were bees for the girls, too. Shira's friends all wanted to study with her.

"But I told them all no," Shira said. She looked at

Reuven. "Guess why?" Reuven looked at her blankly. "It's because my little brother is Mister Lister. That means you're the best one for me to study with. Okay, Reuven?"

Reuven smiled in surprise. Shira wanted to be with him instead of her friends? "Sure," he said, stuffing his mouth with French fries.

For the next three weeks, the house became a Brachot Bee study center. Shira and Reuven tested each other on the lists their teachers gave out. They had to learn which *brachot* to use for different kinds of cookies, cakes, cereals, and candies — for pretzels, popcorn, potato chips, and nuts — for breads, meat, chicken, and fish. They had to learn the *brachot* for different fruits and vegetables. They even had to find out how some things grew in order to know what *brachah* was used for them.

"Strawberries are fruits, aren't they?" Shira argued with Reuven during one study day. "So they should have the same *brachah* as other fruits!"

But Reuven kept shaking his head. "They don't grow on trees like regular fruits. Abba showed me some pictures in the encyclopedia. They grow down on the ground. So they're like vegetables."

On another day, Reuven said he always thought bananas grew on trees.

"No," Shira explained. "Those big fat stalks they grow on aren't trees. I don't remember what they're called. But my science teacher showed us a video of how bananas grow. They're on a kind of bush. So bananas also have the same *brachah* as vegetables."

They went on to study the *brachot* for new clothes and for rainbows, thunder, and lightning. They practiced *brachot* for washing hands first thing in the morning and washing hands before meals. And they memorized *brachot* for Shabbat candles, holiday candles, and for the tall, beautiful Havdalah candle that said farewell to Shabbat.

Reuven and Shira opened the kitchen pantry cabinet and pulled everything out. They lined up all the cans and boxes on the kitchen counters. And they examined ingredients because the *brachot* for things like soups and pancakes depended on what was mixed together in a package. When Reuven picked something up, Shira shouted out the *brachah*. When Shira picked something up, Reuven shouted out the *brachah*. Then Ima came in and told them to put everything away. But they said the *brachot* as they put each item back on its shelf.

Reuven loved the *brachot* lists. Each new one was like a present from school. He loved the way the *brachot* were lined up on the pages. He loved how everything on each list had its matching *brachah*. It was all clear, all laid out neatly. There was no confusion. Reuven could learn and memorize and not worry that he was acting in a way that he wasn't supposed to. Reuven knew exactly what to do. And he knew he could do it well.

Finally, time ran out. Ready or not, the class Brachot Bee day had arrived. Shira and Reuven were silent in the van that morning. They just stared at the houses and trees whizzing past.

"Good luck," Ima said, when she stopped on Maple Avenue. "I'm sure you'll both be great."

"This is it, gang!" Rabbi Goodman said after davening. He rubbed his hands together and smiled. "Don't look so nervous. You all studied, and you'll all do your best."

"But only five of us will win," Amos said.

Rabbi Goodman shook his head. "No, Amos. All twenty of you are already winners." He looked around the room. "Raise your hand if you know why."

Rabbi Goodman called on a boy named David, who rarely volunteered to speak. "Because we learned so many *brachot*," he said softly. "My big brother tested me — he's in high school. He said I know more *brachot* than he does."

"You're absolutely right!" Rabbi Goodman said. "So let's get started. And whether or not you're one of the five..." he looked sternly at them. "I don't want to hear anyone using the word loser."

Chapter 7

# GO, TEAM!

The boys lined up across the front of the room near the board. Rabbi Goodman sat on a chair in front of them. He held a packet of questions.

"I'll ask each of you to tell me the *brachah* for something," Rabbi Goodman explained. "If you don't know it, you'll take your seat."

The first round was easy, Reuven thought. He was sixth in line, next to David. Rabbi Goodman was asking the *brachot* for snacks, things they ate all the time. Reuven said those *brachot* almost every day. He had no trouble giving the answer for potato chips,

41

which was his question. It was *boray pre ha'adamah*, thanking Hashem for creating the foods that grow in the ground.

After the first twenty questions, everyone was still standing. Amos and Levi gave each other high fives.

"Right! Give yourselves a round of applause," Rabbi Goodman said. "I'm really proud of you, and you should all be proud of yourselves." He smiled at them. "Okay. Stretch and shake out your shoulders. Take a deep breath. Here comes Round Two."

This was the fruit and vegetable round, and it was harder. The first boy to sit down gave the wrong *brachot* for a banana. Another had no idea what a kiwi was. A third boy had never eaten cauliflower. By the end of the round, four boys were sitting. They formed a cheering section, clapping when someone answered correctly.

The third round was harder still. The questions were about meat, fish, yogurt, cheese, nuts, and beans. Three more boys sat down, laughing as they joined the cheering section. Thirteen boys were still standing. They moved closer together to fill the empty spaces in the line.

Four more boys sat down in the fourth round. They had given wrong answers about breads, crackers, cakes, pies, pasta, and rice. Three sat down in the fifth round, for questions about candle-lighting and Havdalah.

"Let's take a short break," Rabbi Goodman said, standing up.

The six remaining boys all let out their breath at the same time. Everyone laughed. Reuven looked down the line. David was still next to him, along with Amos, Levi, Tzvi, and a boy named Aharon. Six left.

Other boys seemed to be thinking the same thing that popped into Reuven's mind. Levi asked, "Can't we just have a team of six boys for the school Brachot Bee?"

"I'd love to say yes," Rabbi Goodman said. "But I have to follow the rules. You're all great, but only five can be in the school bee." He stretched and sat down again. "Okay. Round Six. *Brachot* for some more unusual things."

David knew the *brachah* for thunder, and Reuven knew the *brachah* for lightning. But Aharon got stuck on the *brachah* for a rainbow.

"Sorry, Aharon," Rabbi Goodman said gently. "You've been wonderful, but you'll have to sit down. Everyone give him a round of applause."

All the boys clapped and cheered. The five boys still standing grinned at each other. But then Rabbi Goodman said, "There's still one more thing we have to do." The class grew quiet and looked at him. "We need a captain for the team."

"Choose Amos!" someone called out.

"No. It should be Tzvi!" another boy said.

Rabbi Goodman shook his head. He turned to the five remaining boys. "Each of you sit at your desk and take out a pencil and paper. I'm going to ask you to write out the words for a *brachah* that's longer than most and that we don't use very often."

When the boys were ready, Rabbi Goodman said, "Write your name and the full *brachah* for seeing a rainbow." He turned to the rest of the class. "Don't let me hear any hints from anyone who knows it."

The room became very quiet as the five boys sat thinking. Reuven had studied the rainbow *brachah* with Shira, but his mind had gone blank. He looked around at the other boys. The only one writing was David.

"One more minute," Rabbi Goodman said.

Reuven closed his eyes and concentrated. He pictured Shira sitting in the living room testing him on *brachot*. He pictured them emptying and refilling the pantry. Then he pictured a magnificent rainbow in the sky. Suddenly, the *brachah* lists jumped into his mind. He went through the lists in his head as if he were reading them. Then he scribbled down the rainbow *brachah* just as Rabbi Goodman came to collect his paper.

"Let's see," Rabbi Goodman said. He returned to his own desk and sat down. He spread out the five papers. "This one's blank and so is this one. This one has a *brachah*...and it's correct!" He turned to David. "Good job!" He looked down at his desk again. "The next one's blank, and the last one…" He turned to Reuven. "Sorry, Reuven, I can't read your handwriting." Reuven felt sick to his stomach. His handwriting was always a problem. But… "Can you *tell* me the *brachah*, instead?" Rabbi Goodman asked.

Reuven took a shaky breath and closed his eyes. He pictured the lists again. Slowly and carefully, he said, "*Zocher habris, v'ne'eman bivriso, vekayam b'ma'amaro.*" He knew the *brachah* was thanking Hashem for protecting the world. The rainbow was a sign that there would never be a flood as terrible as the one in the time of Noah's Ark.

"Excellent!" Rabbi Goodman exclaimed. He came over to shake Reuven's hand. He shook David's hand, too. "The two of you are the third-grade captains for the school Brachot Bee. Aharon will be an alternate member of the team. That means if someone is sick on the day of the bee, Aharon takes his place."

Supper was like a party that evening. Abba and Ima took Shira and Reuven to the pizza shop to celebrate. Both of them were in the top five of their classes.

"I can't believe Reuven's a captain!" Shira said proudly. She saw her classmate Aviva at another table. Shira called out, "My little brother's one of the third-grade Brachot Bee captains!"

"All that studying paid off," Abba told them with a smile.

"I can still see my pantry spread out all over the counters," Ima laughed. "That better not happen again!"

"It might," Shira teased. "Reuven and I have to study for the school Brachot Bee now."

"And David wants to study with us," Reuven said. His lips were outlined with pizza sauce. "He's the other captain. He wants to know if he can come over on Sunday."

Ima glanced at Abba and smiled. "Of course, he can come over," she said. "You've never had anyone from your class at our house. How about if you invite him to stay for supper?"

The house phone was ringing when they returned home. "It's probably Elisheva," Shira said. "She told me she'd call tonight." She ran into the kitchen to answer it. But then she held out the phone to Reuven. "It's for you," she said, surprised.

Reuven took the phone. He talked for a while about studying for the Brachot Bee on Sunday. After he hung up, Ima asked, "Did you invite David for supper?"

"It wasn't David," Reuven answered. "It was Tzvi. He's also on the team. And he also wants to come here to study on Sunday."

Ima smiled happily. "You can ask Tzvi to stay for supper, too," she said.

The two weeks until the school Brachot Bee raced by. Sometimes Reuven and Shira studied together.

Sometimes they studied with a few teammates. And sometimes they studied in big, noisy groups. David and Tzvi spent the first Sunday at Reuven's house and stayed for supper. Reuven spent the second Sunday at David's house, while Tzvi studied with Levi and Amos at Levi's house.

Chapter 8

# THE BRACHOT BEE

O n the day of the school bee, Reuven and Shira were nervous — they were much more nervous than they had been for their class bees. Neither of them could eat any breakfast.

"You'll be able to think better if you're not hungry," Ima warned. But they still couldn't eat.

"I think I'll throw up if I eat anything," Shira said. Reuven nodded.

They kissed Ima good-bye at school, and Shira said to Reuven, "Good luck, Mister Lister. Your team's going to win."

"So will yours. You know all the *brachot*," Reuven said.

In the middle of the morning, the third and fourth grades filed into the auditorium. The first and second grades had finished their bee and were staying to watch. The older grades would have their Brachot Bee after lunch. There were two semicircles of five chairs each on the stage. Each group of chairs was for each class team.

Everyone took their seats. Rabbi Fine, the principal, congratulated all the students on their hard work preparing for the Brachot Bee. He wished both teams luck. Then he handed each team a marker, an eraser, and a large whiteboard, about the size of their classroom desks.

"These are the rules," he said. "I will ask for a *brachah*. The captains will have two minutes to discuss it with their groups and write an answer on their whiteboard. Make sure someone with good handwriting writes the answers," he added. Everyone laughed.

"See this giant timer?" Rabbi Fine asked. He pointed to a machine on a table in front of him. Reuven thought it was shaped like the small cooking timer Ima used in the kitchen. "A bell will ring when the two minutes are over, and the captains will hold up the boards. If you're correct, Rabbi Goodman will give you a point."

Everyone looked at Rabbi Goodman, who was also

on the stage. He stood next to a large whiteboard on a stand, a marker in his hand. He smiled and waved.

"The first team to score twenty points is the winner," Rabbi Fine continued. "If there's a tie, there will be tiebreaker questions. The only difference is that you'll have only one minute to answer them. Any questions?"

He looked around, but no one raised a hand. "All right, boys. Let's begin!"

The five third-graders looked at each other with nervous smiles. David had the whiteboard on his lap, since he had the best handwriting. Reuven would hold it up, since he was the other captain.

The first questions were easy, just like they had been in the classroom. Both teams scored five points very quickly. But on the sixth question, the fourth-graders mixed up the *brachah* for lightning, giving the one for thunder instead. The third grade had answered the question correctly.

The third-graders in the audience cheered. Their team members onstage grinned at each other. "We're ahead!" Amos whispered.

Both teams answered the next three questions correctly. But question eleven, about the *brachah* for tomato juice, was difficult. Was it *shehakol*, which was the blessing for most drinks? Or was it *ha'adamah*, the blessing for most vegetables?

The boys argued quietly for a full minute about it.

Amos said it was *shehakol* while Reuven was sure it was *ha'adamah*. Amos seemed so certain of his answer that Reuven began to think maybe he was wrong. He closed his eyes and tried to picture the lists, but there was no time. The other boys were worried they wouldn't have an answer before the bell rang. So David wrote down Amos's answer and Reuven held it up — and it was wrong. The fourth-graders cheered when their team's answer of *ha'adamah* was declared correct.

"We should have gone with Reuven's answer," Tzvi whispered. There was no time to think about that, because they all had to listen to question number twelve.

The third- and fourth-graders both neared twenty points. And then they reached twenty — both teams! The two classes broke into loud cheers that echoed off the auditorium walls. Finally, Rabbi Fine held up his *shin* fingers for *sheket*, and the room quieted.

"Congratulations to both teams for a job well done," he said. "I'm tremendously impressed with how well you know the *brachot*!" Everyone applauded, and the boys onstage grinned. "Now for the tiebreaker questions," Rabbi Fine said. "These will be a little more difficult. I'm not going to ask you about a particular food. I'm going to ask you about particular brands of cereal. You'll have to know something about the cereal to get it right."

As Rabbi Fine asked the first question, Reuven

closed his eyes. He pictured himself sitting with Shira at the breakfast table. He could see Ima's *brachot* list as though it were printed on the walls of the auditorium. When he heard Rabbi Fine say, "Rice Chex," he knew the *brachah* was *mezonos*. The other boys agreed with him, and David wrote it quickly on the whiteboard. But when the bell rang after one minute, the fourth-graders had the same answer. It was still a tie.

"You boys are amazing!" Rabbi Fine said with admiration. "We'll need a tougher question to find a winner." He scanned the papers in front of him. "Okay. Here's a pretty new cereal. Let's see if anyone knows the *brachah* for it." He looked around at both teams. "Shooting Stars," he said.

Reuven closed his eyes again. He saw himself across the table from Shira on the first day of school. He pictured his mother picking up the *brachot* list from the kitchen counter. He remembered calling out the *brachah* before his mother could look it up.

"It's *mezonos*. I know it is," Levi whispered.

"No!" Reuven whispered back. He opened his eyes and leaned forward. "I think it's *shehakol*."

The whispered argument went back and forth as the clock ticked down. There was half a minute left. Tzvi said, "Let's go with Reuven's answer. He was right before."

David wrote it down quickly and Reuven held it

up just before the bell rang. The fourth-graders also almost missed the bell. Everyone looked at Rabbi Fine. It seemed to take forever for him to judge their answers. He peered carefully at one whiteboard, then the other. Then he rechecked the answer on his paper. At last he announced that the third-graders' answer was right — and the fourth-graders had it wrong!! The third-graders in the audience began jumping up and down and shouting. Levi, Amos, and even David ran down to celebrate with their classmates. But Tzvi stayed back and walked toward the stage steps with Reuven.

"How do you remember so much?" Tzvi asked over the noise. "What were you doing when you kept closing your eyes?"

Reuven shrugged. "I don't know. I was trying to think — to remember what we studied. When I closed my eyes, it was easier."

"You really knew the brachot," Tzvi said with admiration. "Better than anyone else, even though you didn't seem so sure about it." Then he ran ahead to join the class.

Reuven was about to follow him, when he heard his name. He turned around.

"Congratulations, Reuven," Rabbi Goodman said, holding out his hand.

Reuven took it and shook it hard. Then he

laughed and said, "Oops. I forgot. You only have one right hand." He loosened his grip and shook Rabbi Goodman's hand more gently.

"You did great!" Rabbi Goodman said. "I remember way back on the first day of school. You drew something that looked like a list on your name card. You said your mother had a nickname for you, but I don't remember what it was."

"Mister Lister," Reuven said, smiling broadly. "Because I can remember long lists of things — like *brachot.*"

"You certainly can," Rabbi Goodman agreed. "That's a gift. Your very special talent. Something to be proud of."

Reuven wanted to tell Rabbi Goodman how much he'd enjoyed studying the organized lists of *brachot.* He wanted him to know how much he'd enjoyed the Brachot Bee with all its clear rules. But before he could figure out how to explain it, he heard his name being shouted. People were calling his name, over and over, louder and louder.

"Reu-ven! Reu-ven! Reu-ven!"

Reuven and Rabbi Goodman looked down from the stage. The third-graders stood in a group below them, shouting Reuven's name. Tzvi was waving his arms like an orchestra conductor, leading them in the cheer.

Chapter 9

# ONE OF THE BOYS

**H**anukkah was wonderful for Reuven. There was candle-lighting and presents at home. And there was the pizza and ice cream party in school, with the class cheering their Brachot Bee team. Shira's team had lost to the sixth-grade girls. Still, she enjoyed boasting to her friends about Reuven. She loved that her little brother, Mister Lister, had led his third-grade team to victory.

After Hanukkah, though, the days grew quiet. Reuven no longer sat with the boys on the team at recess and lunch. And at home, he and Shira no longer laughed while testing each other on the *brachot*.

The Recess Races started up again. At first, Reuven felt terrific when the runners kept choosing him to judge the winners. But after a while, Levi and Ephraim were given the job again. Reuven sat alone under the umbrella tree, which was bare now. He watched the runners reach the fence, careful not to get in their way. He continued adding to the winners list in his head.

Then one day David walked slowly over to the tree. He was carrying a large, flat, rectangular box under his arm. "I'm looking for someone to play chess with," he said shyly. "Rabbi Goodman thought I should ask you."

"I don't know how to play chess," Reuven said.

"I can teach you."

Reuven shrugged. "Okay."

They sat on the cold ground under the tree. David opened the box and took out the board. Then he took out the chess pieces. Reuven watched with interest as David set up the game. He put shiny black pieces on one side of the board and shiny white ones on the other. Then he introduced the pieces to Reuven — kings, queens, bishops, knights, castles, and pawns. He explained how each one moved, and Reuven caught on right away.

"It's like a list!" Reuven said with pleasure. "Each piece moves a different way."

They played all recess. David's big brother had

given him papers with the same number of squares as were on the board. David kept them in the game box with a pencil. At the end of recess, Reuven watched David fill in the paper. For each piece on the board, David filled in that square on the paper. He wrote the name of the piece and its color so they could continue their game after lunch. They played on the following day too, and the one after that. And on Sunday, David brought his chess set over to Reuven's house. They played all afternoon.

Reuven loved chess. He loved the orderliness. He loved the many rules. He loved knowing exactly what to do to play the game right. Most of all, he liked spending time with David.

David never got annoyed if Reuven accidentally knocked over some pieces. He wasn't upset if they had to set up the board again. He didn't laugh if Reuven spilled soup on his shirt at supper. And he didn't mind if Reuven spoke too loudly or stood too close. He just waited patiently. He waited for Reuven to remember to lower his voice. He waited for Reuven to take his giant step backward. David just enjoyed being with Reuven, and Reuven enjoyed being with David.

In January, the crisp air made their noses tingle. The air smelled of snow, and frost coated the tree branches. It was too cold for outdoor recess, and the classes played in the gym instead. The giant room was filled with echoing noise. It shook from all the running feet and bouncing balls. All this upset Reuven at first. He hated to even step into the gym. He wanted to run out into the hallway and cover his ears with his hands. But then he and David took over one corner of the gym. There, out of the way, they could set up their game. Reuven could concentrate only on the board. He could shut out the shouting and the pounding around him. He could ignore the wildness that he found so disturbing.

One day, they looked up to see Tzvi watching them. "My father plays chess," he told them. "He says it's a game that can sharpen your brain."

David laughed in his shy way. "It's fun," he said, and Reuven nodded in agreement.

"Can you teach me?" Tzvi asked. He sat down cross-legged on the floor near the board.

"Sure," David said. He and Reuven explained the rules to him as they continued their game.

Tzvi caught on almost as quickly as Reuven had. Now Tzvi also played at most recesses and during lunch. Reuven began keeping another win list in his head. This one wasn't for Recess Races. It was for chess victories.

Sometimes Rabbi Goodman came to their corner to watch. "My grandfather taught me chess when I was your age," he told them. "I used to love to play with him."

Once Tzvi had joined "the chess corner," Amos and

Levi weren't far behind. They were curious about what was going on. "Can you teach us to play, too?" they asked.

David and Reuven became the captains of the Third Grade Chess Club. David was in charge of the game and its tracking sheets. Reuven impressed everyone by keeping the winners list in his head. But there was only one game board for five club members. That meant three boys watched while two boys played, and the corner of the gym got crowded. One day, Tzvi was playing against David. Reuven returned from the bathroom and found Amos and Levi blocking his view. He started squeezing between them to see the game.

"Stop pushing me!" Levi muttered. He elbowed Reuven away from him. Reuven lost his balance and fell into Amos. Amos fell onto the game board. Chess pieces scattered everywhere.

"Look what you made me do!" Amos yelled. He pushed Reuven. Reuven stumbled into the path of two boys racing by. They crashed into Reuven and sent him sprawling.

"What's going on here?" Rabbi Goodman cried out. He helped Reuven up.

"He's always pushing people!" Levi complained. "He never listens if you tell him to stop."

"And he shoved me into the game board," Amos put in. "The whole game's messed up now!"

Rabbi Goodman turned to Reuven, who was clearly

upset. "Let's go someplace quiet to talk this over," he said gently. But before leaving with Reuven, he turned back to Amos and Levi. "I'll be talking to the two of you afterward," he said.

*It's like the first day of school again*, Reuven thought. Again, he climbed the steps with Rabbi Goodman. Again, they entered the resource room. Mrs. Silver smiled at Reuven. Then she left him and Rabbi Goodman in peace, at the table in the corner. It was just like the first time. But now, the walls were decorated with posters for *Tu B'Shevat*, the Jewish New Year for the Trees. And the room was warm, the windows closed tightly against the cold. Even so, Reuven shivered. All he'd wanted to do was be part of the group. It just never seemed to work out.

Chapter 10

# ONE MORE LIST

"Tell me what happened down there," Rabbi Goodman said. Like last time, they sat facing each other.

"I couldn't see the game," Reuven said, gulping down a sob. "I wanted to watch, but there was no room."

"So you tried to squeeze between Amos and Levi?" asked Rabbi Goodman.

Reuven nodded. He took a shaky breath and stared at the floor. "I forgot to just ask them to move," he mumbled. He looked up. "Are we going to act it out, like we did the first day of school?"

Rabbi Goodman smiled. "Do you think we have to?"

Reuven thought for a minute and shook his head.

"I agree," Rabbi Goodman said. "You know how to act, Reuven. You just forgot this time, that's all."

Reuven thought about that. He said, "I think Levi and Amos forgot, too."

"That's very true, and I'll be talking to them about it. But I wanted to talk to you first, because you looked so upset. Was it just because you were pushed and fell?"

"Yes," Reuven whispered.

"Are you sure?" Rabbi Goodman asked carefully.

Reuven stared at the table. Then suddenly he burst out loudly, "Something always goes wrong!" He was doing all he could not to cry.

Rabbi Goodman nodded. "It certainly feels that way sometimes," he agreed. "We try and try, and things go wrong anyway. That hurts a lot."

Rabbi Goodman fell silent and the two of them sat without speaking. Reuven kept thinking about the Chess Club — how good it used to make him feel, and now how terrible it made him feel. It made the day seem gray and dreary, even though the winter sun was shining outside.

"Reuven," Rabbi Goodman said at last. He sounded a little sad. "What happened to you today...it happens to other people, too. We all want everything to work out right for us. But sometimes it doesn't. And something like it might happen again. A lot of things can go wrong."

Reuven stared down at the table again. He slumped in his chair and his shoulders drooped. He couldn't stop thinking about being pushed away from the chess game. Then he heard Rabbi Goodman start speaking again.

"Reuven," Rabbi Goodman said. "Things can go wrong. But thinking back to the first time I met you, last September...I think a lot has gone right for you, too." Rabbi Goodman let Reuven consider that for a minute. Then he asked, "Reuven, what's that nickname your mother gave you?"

Reuven looked at him, confused. "You mean, Mister Lister?"

Rabbi Goodman nodded. "Because you like lists, and you remember them. It's one of the things that makes you special. It's a talent, your wonderful gift." He smiled at Reuven. "We're going to make a list together right now, Reuven. And it's important for you to learn it and remember it. Okay?"

Reuven shrugged. "I guess so," he said slowly.

Rabbi Goodman asked Mrs. Silver for a sheet of paper and a pencil. Then he wrote at the top of it:

Reuven's List of Things That Went Right

"Let's begin," Rabbi Goodman said. "We'll start with the first day of school. What's the first thing you learned in my class?"

Reuven thought back to the first day. He remembered the name cards, the riddles, and the Recess Race. "I learned to take a giant step backward," he said.

"Good," Rabbi Goodman said. "We'll put that first on the list." He wrote it on the paper. "What's next?"

Reuven sat up in his chair and straightened his shoulders. Together he and Rabbi Goodman talked through all the months of third grade so far. When they were finished, Rabbi Goodman showed Reuven the list.

Reuven read:

- I learned to take a giant step backward.

- I was a captain in the Brachot Bee.

- I learned to hug Ima and Abba without hurting them.

- Shira wanted to study the brachot with me instead of with her friends.

- I learned to speak more quietly.

- I became friends with David and Tzvi.

- I learned to shake hands without squeezing too hard.

- I started a chess club with David.

"That's a pretty good start," Rabbi Goodman said. "You have to memorize it. I know you can do that!

And that way, whenever things go wrong, you'll have a plan. You'll close your eyes and picture every item on this list."

Reuven read the list again. It made him smile. He wanted to tell Rabbi Goodman how good the list made him feel, but he didn't know how. He wanted to thank Rabbi Goodman for other things, too. But he didn't know how to put it into words. Then he had an idea. "Can I add something?" he asked.

"Absolutely!" Rabbi Goodman said. "This is your own private list. It's very important that you add to it every time something goes right."

"I want to put this at the top of the list," Reuven said. "It needs to be the first thing under 'Things That Went Right.'"

He took the pencil from Rabbi Goodman and wrote as neatly as he could:

- I came to Rabbi Goodman's class for third grade.

# APPENDIX
## ABOUT *BRACHOT* (BLESSINGS)

**W**hen we get presents we say "Thank You." That's what *brachot* are all about. They are a way of saying to God that we appreciate all the great presents we have in our world.

All the *brachot* begin with words that have this meaning:

"God, blessings come from You, You are our God, and You are king of the world."

Other words are added on, depending on what food a person is going to eat or what a person is doing.

Each *brachah* has a code word. It's the name of the *brachah*. In the Brachot Bee, David only had to write the code word on the white board, and Rabbi Fine knew which *brachah* he meant.

### REUVEN'S LIST OF FAVORITE BRACHOT

We all love some presents better than others. *Reuven's List of Favorite Brachot* is for the presents he loves best in the world.

**CANDY**: Especially chocolate bars and giant lollipops. Reuven loves this *brachah*, because it's for most candies and drinks.

Code Word: Shehakol

Brachah: *Shehakol niheyeh bidvaro* – All things are created by God.

**COOKIES AND CAKES**: Chocolate chip cookies and birthday cakes are the best.

Code Word: Mezonot

Brachah: *Boray minay mezonot* – God creates all types of foods.

**ICE CREAM**: Reuven's favorite has a caramel swirl.

Code Word: *Shehakol* – just like the brachah for candy.

Brachah: *Shehakol niheyeh bidvaro* - All things are created by God.

**FRUIT**: Peaches with whipped cream is a special treat in Reuven's house.

Code Word: Ha'etz

Brachah: *Boray pre ha'etz* – God creates the fruit of the tree.

**VEGETABLES**: Especially cauliflower with the spices Ima uses.

Code Word: Ha-adamah

Brachah: *Boray pre ha'adamah* – God creates the fruit of the ground.

**LASAGNA**: Yum!!

Code Word: Mezonot – just like the brachah for

cookies and cakes, because lasagna noodles are also made from flour.

Brachah: *Boray minay mezonot* – God creates all types of foods.

# ACKNOWLEDGMENTS

I would like to thank my sister Barbara, who first suggested writing this type of story and provided invaluable psychological insights. Great thanks also to my sister Joyce for her educational suggestions, unflagging support, and encouragement.

Special acknowledgment to all of my children and their families for their very helpful critiques, particularly Shua, my partner in writing.

I am grateful beyond measure to Altie Karper, editorial director of Schocken Books, for her advice and support, and to publishing consultant Paula Breen.

Very heartfelt thanks to Esther Heller, editor in chief of Menucha Publishers, for shepherding me through this process so capably, to Cindy Scarr for her careful editing, to Daliya Shapiro for her proofreading, and to Sarah Zee for the delightful and compassionate illustrations that brought my characters to life.

Above all, thank you to my husband, Bob, who always believes in me and never lets me give up.

# ABOUT THE AUTHOR

Judith Pransky has been teaching young children, teenagers, and adults for years, and has known many students like Reuven and his classmates. She has also been fortunate to become acquainted with talented and compassionate teachers like Rabbi Goodman. Her degrees are in English, History, and Education, and she has written feature articles for newspapers. She and her husband live near Philadelphia and enjoy traveling around the United States and to Israel to visit their children and grandchildren.